BATTLE OF
THE BANDS

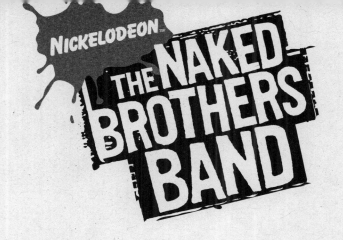

NICKELODEON™

THE NAKED BROTHERS BAND

BATTLE OF THE BANDS

Adapted by Michael Anthony Steele
Based on "Battle of the Bands Part 1"
and "Battle of the Bands Part 2"
written by Will McRobb & Chris Viscardi

Based on *The Naked Brothers Band* created by Polly Draper

SCHOLASTIC INC.

New York   Toronto   London   Auckland   Sydney
Mexico City   New Delhi   Hong Kong   Buenos Aires

ISBN-10: 0-545-03921-5
ISBN-13: 978-0-545-03921-5

Published by Scholastic Inc.
SCHOLASTIC and associated logos are trademarks and/or registered trademarks of Scholastic Inc.

12 11 10 9 8 7 6 5 4 3 2   8 9 10/0

Printed in the U.S.A.
First printing, January 2008

BATTLE OF THE BANDS

Nat jammed on his keyboard while the rest of the Naked Brothers Band played behind him. They performed in their personal studio in New York City in front of a green screen. The special backdrop let them use a computer to insert any background they wanted. This time, the computer displayed images from a city on the other side of the country — Los Angeles. The pictures fit perfectly with the title of Nat's new song, "L.A." He sang the chorus.

L.A. L.A. L.A. L.A. go today
L.A. L.A. L.A. L.A. it's a date
L.A. L.A. L.A. L.A. say hoorah

Nat and his brother Alex founded the Naked Brothers Band many years ago. After a couple of name changes and even more personnel changes, they ended up with the current line-up. Nat was the lead vocalist, played keyboard, and wrote most of the songs. He shook his head as he sang, making his short brown hair flap back and forth — Beatles-style. Alex's curly hair was shoved under his red, white, and blue bandanna. His tattoo-covered arms were a blur as he played the drums. He sang backup vocals as well.

Sunshine happiness in Studio City
Pool out back,
Yard out front
Happy dogs happy dogs

Rosalina tapped a foot as she played her thumping bass guitar. Her long brown hair was pulled back into a ponytail. Qaasim's dreadlocks whipped around as his fingers raced up the neck of his guitar. He played lead guitar and really knew how to rock.

L.A. L.A. L.A. L.A. go today
L.A. L.A. L.A. L.A. it's a date
L.A. L.A. L.A. L.A. say hoorah

Thomas ran his bow across the cello strings. An unusual instrument for a rock band, his cello added another unique tone to their music. David pushed up his glasses between forming chords on his auxiliary keyboard. Like Thomas and Nat, he was eleven years old. Alex was eight, Qassim was ten, and Rosalina was thirteen. Everyone sang back-up vocals as well.

Sunshine City going around
Oh wow the flu is getting me down

How can you live in the rain or snow
When you can live in L.A.

Two cameramen videotaped the band as they performed. Mohammed moved his camera closer to Nat. Ken aimed his at Alex. The band wasn't shooting a music video. They were just rehearsing. However, Ken and Mohammed had been following them around for several weeks. They filmed almost every aspect of the Naked Brothers Band's lives for a TV series.

L.A. L.A. makes your troubles go away
L.A. L.A. it's the day
L.A. L.A. why's everyone going away

As they came out of the second chorus, someone played something wrong and several sour notes clashed. Everyone stopped and looked at each other, bursting into laughter.

Nat looked into Mohammed's camera lens. "Sorry about that," he said. "We wanted to sing you a song that's brand new. I mean, really brand new."

Alex turned to Ken's camera. "It's so brand new that it came fresh out of Nat's song-baking oven last night."

"Now you understand why we messed up," added Thomas.

Alex raised a hand. "Actually, it was me."

Rosalina smiled. "Oh good, I thought it was me."

"Sure, take all the credit," Nat joked. "I'm the one who forgot to come in on that third bar."

"Anyway, it was an experiment," Rosalina told the cameras. "We thought that if we sang it in front of the green screen they could put all of these beautiful images of L.A. in later. It would distract you from the fact that we might mess up."

"Yeah," Qaasim agreed. "So by the time you'd see this, you'd be watching beautiful pictures of sunsets and beaches and stuff and not listening to the song at all."

"Yes, that's always been my goal," said Nat. "To write songs that you'll not listen to at all." Everyone laughed. Nat placed his hand above the keyboard and turned to the others. "Should we try again?"

Everyone agreed and Alex began with a powerful drum roll. The band rehearsed the song until they got it right.

After rehearsal, everyone gathered back at Nat and Alex's apartment. The place was decorated as you would expect a pre-teen rock group's apartment to be decorated. Colorful paint covered the walls. Large futuristic furniture was scattered about. And other distractions like a jukebox, punching bag, and baby grand piano were included. Mohammed and Ken were there as well, using the colorful apartment as a background for their footage.

The band was busy signing CDs for the upcoming Little Kids Rock charity event. The Naked Brothers Band was sharing the event with another band called the L.A. Surfers. They were a few years older than Nat and played harder rock music. A few of the Surfers' CDs were scattered about the coffee table.

Cooper helped them organize the stacks of CDs. At the age of eleven, Cooper was the band's manager. He always wore a suit, tie, and large-rimmed glasses. He was very professional. "Here, make it so they can read your name." He handed one of the L.A. Surfer CDs to Alex. "Like this."

Alex examined it. "I can't believe the L.A. Surfers signed a thousand of these for the charity gig."

Nat pointed to a signature on the CD cover. "And look at Bobby Love's signatures. Each one is perfect. How does he do that?"

Qaasim leaned in. "Whoa. Look at that. How does he make his L's loop like that?"

Alex tossed the CD back onto the pile. "And every single one is like that. I've checked."

Nat leaned back to look at David and Thomas. They played a game of air hockey as they signed. "You guys shouldn't play while you're signing," said Nat. "We want our autographs to look as good as Bobby Love's."

"Don't worry," said Thomas. "We have a technique." He knocked the puck into David's goal then signed a CD.

David signed a CD then reset the puck. "I can't believe the L.A. Surfers are doing a charity gig at all."

"Why?" asked Rosalina.

"They're so tough and leather jacket-ish," said Thomas. "They don't seem like the type."

"What?" asked Nat. "You have to be wimps like us to want to help people?"

David shrugged. "Kinda. Yeah."

Rosalina signed another CD. "I don't think it's strange they're doing it. I heard Bobby Love is a really great guy."

"Of course *you've* heard that," said Thomas. He slammed another puck home then signed another CD.

Rosalina put her marker down. "What's that supposed to mean?"

"Ooh, I just *looove* the Bobby Love lover boy," Thomas said in a high-pitched voice.

"She does not," said Nat. He turned back to Rosalina. "Do you?"

She frowned. "No, I don't."

Nat had a huge crush on Rosalina. Unfortunately, it wasn't much of a secret. The entire band knew about it, and many of their fans talked about it on the message boards and blogs. And even though she was a bit older than him, he kind of thought she felt the same way.

David rolled his eyes. "Her screensaver has his picture with hearts around him."

Nat's heart sank. "No it doesn't," he told David. He turned back to her. "Does it?"

Rosalina cringed. "Yeah, but . . ."

"But?" asked Thomas.

"But, I don't love Bobby Love," she said. Then she turned to Nat. "I just . . . respect him as a musician."

"Yeah, you guys," said Nat. "She just respects him as a musician." He turned back to Rosalina once again. "Why?"

"Why what?" asked Rosalina.

"Why do you respect him as a musician?" asked Nat.

Rosalina glanced around nervously. All eyes were on her. "Because he's really good. I mean, the band is good. The songs are . . ." She picked up a CD. "His handwriting is really, really . . ." She leaped to her feet and ran at Thomas and David. "Why were you looking at my computer anyway?" The two laughed as she chased them around the apartment.

That night, after everyone left, Nat and Alex logged on to Bobby Love's official website. The introduction animation showed Bobby Love talking directly to camera. "Thank you for being a fan. I'm Bobby and . . . I love you."

Bobby Love oozed cool. He spoke in an English accent, wore a leather jacket, and had shades of orange mixed into his spiked hair. Dark eyeliner encircled his eyes, and tattoos adorned his arms. Nat didn't know if they were real tattoos or fake ones like the ones Alex had. Either way, it worked for Bobby Love. The girls went crazy for him.

"I am so doomed," said Nat. "When Rosalina meets him tomorrow at the photo shoot, she's never gong to look at me again."

Alex scrolled through some of the images on the site. "Wow! Here's a picture of Bobby playing guitar, riding a motorcycle, drinking coffee, and surfing all at once."

Nat sighed. Sure enough, there was a photo of Bobby Love doing all those things. It had obviously been digitally manipulated (how can you drink coffee on a surfboard?) but it didn't make the image look any less cool.

Alex laughed. "You can't even read while riding in a car."

Nat shook his head. "Thanks for reminding me."

Their dad entered the room holding his accordion. Like his sons, Mr. Wolff was a musician, too. However, his music career mostly consisted of playing accordion at a German restaurant down the street. Either way, he was a great father and supported his sons in their rock-stardom. He sat down next to them and polished his accordion with a small towel.

"Oh, and you don't have an English accent," Alex added. "Another friendly reminder."

"Thanks," said Nat.

Alex smiled. "Hey, remember when you used to fake an English accent to impress Rosalina?"

Before Rosalina joined the band, Nat would only speak to her in a phony accent. He was always very nervous whenever he talked to her. It sounded really lame, but it was all he could think to do. It took a long time to break that stupid habit.

"Maybe you should go back to doing that," said Alex. "I'm just saying, you can't underestimate the charms of the English. Pip-pip, old chap!"

Mr. Wolff leaned over and glanced at the computer screen. "This Bobby Love guy is the one who should worry about Nat," he said "I mean, you are the *Girl Magnet*." Nat got that nickname because most of the group's female fans flocked to him more than any other member of the band.

Nat shook his head. "Then Bobby Love must be the *Girl Vacuum Cleaner*."

"You could start with drinking coffee," Alex suggested. "Then work your way up to surfing."

"I know you'll just call me corny old dad for saying this, but you've just got to be yourself," said Mr. Wolff. "That's how I got Betty to be my honey bunny." Their father had recently started dating a woman named Betty. They even formed a band called the Honey Bunnies.

He played a chord on his accordion and began to sing:

She thought I was a rock star,
Then saw I'm a dad named Sonny.
Now she's my honey bunny!

Mr. Wolff beamed. "That sounded good. I might be onto a new song here!"

As their dad continued to play, Alex covered his head with a pillow. Nat didn't pay attention to the loud accordion. He only stared at the picture of Bobby Love. He got an idea and smiled.

The next morning, Nat decided to ride his bike to the photo shoot. He'd also decided to change his look a bit. Unfortunately, sporting his new look was much harder than he thought. His leather jacket flapped in the breeze and the cold morning air shot through the holes in his T-shirt. He had difficulty seeing through the smoked visor of the motorcycle helmet. He also had trouble holding the hot cup of coffee and the handlebars at the same time. Bobby Love must practice a lot to make it look so easy.

When he pulled up to the studio, Rosalina was chaining her bike to an iron fence. Ken was there as well, videotaping her. Nat pulled up beside her and carefully dismounted his bike, trying carefully not to spill his coffee. He then slowly removed his helmet, attempting to avoid ripping off the sunglasses underneath. He revealed his new spiked hairdo, complete with orange streaks. He didn't say a word to Rosalina. He simply nodded casually.

"What happened to your hair?" she asked.

"I have no idea," he said coolly. "I woke up this morning and 'Hello, orange!' Talk about a wild night." He lowered his sunglasses. "Wait. Is it morning?"

"You said you were going to bed early last night," said Rosalina.

"Not me," he replied. "I'll sleep when I'm dead. Know what I mean?"

"No," replied Rosalina. She glanced down at the cup in his hand. "And since when do you drink coffee?"

"Coffee?" Nat held up the cup. "This is a latte. And I like it a lot . . . tay." Nat took a sip of the drink and nearly choked as the scalding, bitter liquid filled his mouth.

Rosalina cocked her head. "You're acting really weird, Nat."

"It's no act. This is the real me," he said. "The Wolff-man. Livin' *la vida loca*!"

Rosalina stared at him a moment longer. Suddenly, she grinned and glanced around. "Wait. I'm being punked, aren't I? This is all some joke, right?" She pointed at Ken. "For the cameras."

"No, this is the real me, Rosalina," said Nat. "I'm bad to the bone."

She playfully gave him a shove. "Nat Wolff, you are

so *not* bad to the bone." She walked up the steps to the studio. "I can't believe it. You totally punked me!"

Nat groaned in frustration. He locked up his bike and went inside. He didn't join the rest of the band, however. He darted straight to the men's room, turned on the water in the sink, and began to wash the orange out of his hair. Ken followed him. For once, he wished he wasn't part of a TV series.

Alex walked in. "How'd it go?" he asked. "Does she love you now that you're Bobby Love–ish?"

"She thought it was a joke," replied Nat. He grabbed another handful of water and scrubbed harder. "She's still laughing at me."

"I told you the orange hair might be one step beyond," said Alex.

"Alex will you help me get it out of my hair before the photo shoot?" asked Nat.

Alex pulled a paper towel from the dispenser and wet it. "Bobby Love hasn't come yet. Don't worry."

Nat took the paper towel and wiped at another orange streak. "I give up, anyway. I can't compete with a guy who surfs and rides a motorcycle. I just can't."

"True," Alex agreed.

"I'm going to take Dad's advice and just be myself." He scrubbed harder. "Bobby Love is probably a really nice guy. We already know he cares about kids because he's doing this Little Kids Rock charity, right?"

"I guess," replied Alex.

"So I'll just be his friend and then I can ask him questions about L.A. and England and how to swallow coffee without gagging." He looked at his reflection in the mirror. "Is it coming out yet?"

Alex leaned closer. "Not really." He reached down and pulled up a toilet brush. "Maybe we should try this."

Nat frowned. "I don't think so."

Alex chuckled. "Just trying to be helpful."

Nat wet his hands some more. "Don't you think that's a good idea though, Alex?"

"What?" asked Alex.

"To become Bobby's really good friend and then he won't want to steal my girlfriend," Nat replied.

"Sure," said Alex. "But I just want to point out that she's not actually your girlfriend."

Nat sighed. "Yeah, I'm aware of that."

"Friendly reminder," said Alex.

Suddenly, they heard a voice just outside the restroom door. "Be right with you. Just going to hit the loo." That someone had a very thick English accent.

"Somebody's coming," said Nat. "Hide."

"What's the difference?" asked Alex. He looked at Ken and his camera. "You're already on camera."

"That's Bobby Love's voice," Nat replied. "I don't want him to see me orange like this."

Nat ran to one of the toilet stalls and pushed open the door. He ushered in Alex and Ken, then closed the door behind them. Through the gap around the stall door, he saw Bobby Love enter the men's room. The older boy looked in the mirror and began to adjust his hair. Then his cell phone rang. Bobby pulled it out of his leather jacket and held it up to his ear.

"Bobby Love loves you," he said.

After a long pause, Bobby replied. Oddly enough, he no longer had an English accent. "Dude, you were right. This bogus little charity gig is going to get the band a ton of press. You should see them out there. It's like feeding time at the zoo."

"He's not English," whispered Alex.

Nat couldn't believe it. Not only was he not English, he sounded like one of those surfer dudes.

Bobby listened as the other caller spoke. Then he replied. "Dude, don't surf today, man. You have to write me a new hit." Bobby Love laughed. "Another Bobby Love original. I can't keep cranking on this same tired stuff you wrote earlier."

Nat's eyes widened. He whispered to Alex. "He doesn't even write his own songs."

Bobby Love's voice raised. "No excuses, dude! Dig this. I just heard this kid Nat Wolff has written twenty-two new songs. I mean this little punk is like nine or ten years old."

"I'm eleven," whispered Nat.

"His bass player is hot, though," said Bobby. "I think I'll hit on her."

Nat burned with anger. "I'm going to kill him."

Bobby Love glanced down at the sink and took a step back. "Whoa, this place is rank. The sink is filled with orange water, man. It's nasty."

Just then, one of Bobby Love's band members entered the restroom. "Oh man, I drank too much punch," he said. "I have to go." He walked straight toward their stall. Before he grabbed the handle, he turned to Bobby. "They want you out there, man."

Bobby continued to talk on the phone. "Pork just walked in. Yeah, I have to slide now." He chuckled again. "Time to do my whole Bobby Love snow job." He paused for a reply then frowned. "Dude, write some new stuff or I'll fire you, man. I'm serious!"

The guy named Pork tried to open the stall door. Nat hoped the little latch would hold as Pork rattled it back and forth.

"Okay, I'm sorry; don't quit on me. Don't quit on me," Bobby spoke into the phone. "I was just yanking your chain, man."

Bobby hung up the phone and looked at Pork. "Dude, is someone in there?"

"I guess so," said Pork.

Bobby's eyes widened. "We've got to get out of here!"

"I have to go," said Pork.

"Hold it in, man," said Bobby. He stared at the stall door as he shoved his bandmate out the restroom door.

Once they were gone, Nat, Alex, and Ken stepped out of the stall. "Okay, that was surprising," said Nat.

"Yeah," agreed Alex.

Nat peaked out of the men's room door. Bobby Love and his band stood in front of the photo studio's white background. The rest of the Naked Brothers Band was there as well.

As the photographer and his crew prepared for the shoot, Bobby and his band chatted with a couple of reporters. Nat motioned for Alex and Ken to exit. Once they were out, Nat did the same. However, as he left, Bobby Love looked over and caught his eye. He smiled and Nat glared back. Nat was sure Bobby knew that he was the one in the restroom. He glared a bit longer. He wanted Bobby to know that he heard everything.

They joined the rest of the Naked Brothers Band as they stood on the sidelines, waiting for the shoot. Nat sidled next to Rosalina. She stared up at Bobby Love. She stared a little too much as far as Nat was concerned.

"It's not about publicity, mate," said Bobby Love. His English accent was back and turned up to eleven. "It's about the kids. It's about some seven-year-old out there who wants to play the trumpet, or the flute, or the . . ."

"Radio!" suggested Pork. Everyone laughed, thinking Pork had made a joke. Pork glanced around then laughed as well. He didn't seem too bright.

Bobby Love finished his speech. "It's about using the power of music to put music in the hands of our greatest resource — kids."

"That is so sweet," said Rosalina. Then she looked over and noticed Nat standing beside her. "Nat, where have you been? Bobby Love has been saying the most incredible things."

Nat rolled his eyes. "I'll bet he has. You should have heard the incredible things he said in the bathroom."

"What are you talking about?" asked Rosalina.

Nat leaned closer. "He's a huge phony. Huge," he whispered. "You won't believe it."

Rosalina looked at Ken's camera and smiled. "What? Are you punking me again?"

Bobby Love appeared between Nat and Rosalina. "There's my mate." He put an arm around Nat's shoulders and looked back at the press. "The talented Nat Wolff. I admire this man so much." He leaned close and whispered into Nat's ear, his English accent gone, "So you were the one spying on me."

"I wasn't spying," Nat said through clenched teeth.

"A liar and a spyer," whispered Bobby. "You better not say anything." He turned toward Rosalina. His accent returned. "Hello, gorgeous Rosalina." He elbowed Nat in the ribs, a little too hard. "You're a lucky man, mate, getting to play music with her all day."

Rosalina beamed up at him. "I just want to say that I admire you so much, and I love what you just said about Little Kids Rock."

Bobby smiled. "The children are our future, Rosalina."

"Yes," she agreed. "Yes, they are."

Bobby Love waved the press closer. "Can I get a picture with Rosalina? I'm a big fan."

A young girl pushed her way through the crowd. She wore thin glasses and her hair was pulled back in a bun. Although she looked a year younger than Nat, she had an air of authority about her. "Yes! Let's get some pictures!" She ushered both bands back to the white backdrop. Once they were in position, she extended a hand toward Nat.

"How do you do, by the way? I'm Patty, the representative for Little Kids Rock." She shook Bobby's hand as well. "Thank you both for coming. Do you need me to say that in other languages? Because I'm president of the Mandarin club at school. Chinese is the new Spanish, you know."

As the shoot got underway, Bobby Love positioned himself so he stood next to Rosalina. "Now that I've got you cornered, Rosalina, tell me, on 'Banana Smoothie,' is that a C7 you're playing?"

"Yeah, it's a C7," said Rosalina.

Bobby winked at her. "That is so cheeky."

Nat scoffed and rolled his eyes.

Bobby Love leaned forward. "Did you say something, Nate?"

"It's Nat," he replied. "And I hardly think a C7 is cheeky. D flat, maybe."

Rosalina wasn't even listening. Meanwhile, Alex was busy comparing tattoos with the L.A. Surfers' drummer.

"I got that one in Reno," said the drummer as he pointed to a snake on his arm. "This one in Shanghai." He pointed out a panther. "And this one . . . actually, I've never even seen that one before." He gestured to Alex's arm. "Where are yours from?"

"A cereal box," said Alex.

Nat wedged himself between Bobby and Rosalina. "So, Bobby, where in England are you actually from? Your accent is very unusual."

Bobby held a hand to one ear. "Sorry, mate?"

"It's not Nate," Nat barked.

"He said *mate*," Rosalina corrected.

"Oh," he said.

Bobby pushed himself past Nat to move closer to Rosalina. "Nat, would you mind if I took your lady for a spin on my motor bike after this?"

"Yeah, I'd mind," said Nat.

"I'm not his lady." She glared at Nat then smiled at Bobby. "And I'd love to take a ride with you, Bobby."

"You can't ride a motorcycle with him," said Nat.

"Why not?" asked Rosalina.

"You just can't," he replied.

"Oh, yes I can," said Rosalina.

"Settle down there, Nate," said Bobby Love.

"I'm not your mate," Nat growled.

Rosalina glared at Nat. "He said *Nate*."

Nat decided he didn't want to anger Rosalina anymore than he already had. He moved back to join Alex. "She's falling for him."

"Did you tell her he's a phony baloney?" asked Alex.

"I tried to," replied Nat. "But he swooped in and told her that her C7 was cheeky, and now she doesn't care what I say."

Nat watched as Bobby and Rosalina chatted back and forth. Every time Rosalina laughed, Nat's heart sank a little lower.

After the shoot, Bobby Love ushered Rosalina to the street outside. He didn't say much because his mind was on what happened in the men's room. He worried about what Nat had overheard. If Nat spilled the beans about his phony act, it would be all over for the L.A. Surfers. Luckily, Nat seemed like too much of a goody-goody to snitch on him.

Bobby also had Rosalina in his corner. Everyone that followed the Naked Brothers Band knew that Nat had a huge crush on her, so Bobby decided to keep flirting with her to help keep Nat in line. Things couldn't have turned out better if he'd planned it.

When they got to his motorcycle, Rosalina seemed to be impressed (as all girls were). Yet, something seemed to be troubling her. "I don't know why Nat's acting like this," she said. "He's usually the nicest guy in the world."

Bobby put on his serious face. "Jealousy is a destructive emotion, Rosalina," he explained in his smooth English accent. "And have you ever noticed that the word *lousy* is in the word *jealousy*?" This line worked every time. "That's because jealousy makes you feel lousy."

"I guess so . . ." said Rosalina. She still seemed upset.

Okay, so that line didn't work as well on Rosalina as it did on most girls. Oh, well. He'd put her on the back of his bike and take her for a spin. He knew he would eventually be able to charm her, and she'd fall for him just like all the others. Once she fell for him, Nat would be too devastated to cause any trouble.

"Are you ready for your ride?" he asked.

"Okay," she replied.

He helped her onto his motorcycle, and they sped down the street.

After the photo shoot, everyone met at the Naked Brothers Band's music studio. Rosalina still wasn't back from her motorcycle ride with Bobby Love. However, Nat immediately told everyone else what he and Alex had discovered. They gathered around Ken and his video camera. On the camera's tiny monitor, they watched the scene from the men's room. Jesse, their babysitter and tutor was there too. Even she got to see what a big fake Bobby Love was.

"Has Rosalina seen this?" asked Thomas.

"She wouldn't believe it," Nat replied. "She'd just think she was being *punked* again."

Qaasim shook his head. "It's a proven scientific fact. Girls always fall for phonies."

"I don't," Jesse proclaimed. She tucked a loose strand of her brown hair behind one ear. "I believe you guys."

Alex put an arm around Jesse. "That's my girl." Alex believed that Jesse was his girlfriend. It didn't matter that she was in her twenties and dated other guys. He still believed it.

"Yeah, I've been suspicious of Bobby Love for a long time now," she added.

"You have?" asked Nat.

"Oh, yeah." Her face became serious. "I used to be a walking Bobby Love encyclopedia until I found out he's not who he says he is."

"What did you find out?" asked David.

"In the first place, I found out he doesn't sign his own name on autographs," she explained. "He stamps them on."

"I knew it!" yelled Nat.

"That's why each autograph looks the same," said Thomas.

"That's why the loops on those L's look so perfect," added Qaasim.

"An autograph stamp!" shouted Alex. "Good idea. I have to get one of those."

Jesse wasn't finished. "And then I found out his real name isn't even Bobby."

Everyone leaned forward. "What is it?"

Jesse glanced around as if checking to see if the coast was clear. When she was satisfied, she leaned closer. "It's Robert," she whispered.

The boys glanced at each other. Nat didn't know if they should tell Jesse that *Bobby* or *Bob* is short for the name *Robert*. He decided not to be the one to break it to her.

"Anything else?" he asked.

Jesse thought for a moment. "That was probably the biggest thing."

"Oh," said Nat.

"That and the fact that he's afraid of balloons," she added.

The guys glanced at each other then burst into laughter. "Afraid of balloons?" asked Nat.

"No way!" shouted David.

"What kind of a wimp is afraid of balloons?" asked Thomas.

Qaasim slapped Nat on the back. "He's afraid of balloons, man. You owe it to Rosalina to let her know."

Later that day, when Rosalina finally arrived, Nat tried to explain everything. He told her how Bobby Love wasn't really English, didn't write his own songs, and that he was even afraid of balloons. She didn't believe any of it.

"What kind of wimp is afraid of balloons?" asked Nat.

"Nat, do you realize you're being ridiculous?" asked Rosalina.

"If you had only watched the video of him in the bathroom, you wouldn't think so," said Nat.

Rosalina grimaced. "Eww, no. I would think you were really creepy for spying on him."

"For the last time, I wasn't spying. I was hiding," said Nat.

"Why can't you just deal with the fact that Bobby is the real thing?" she asked. "He's really English. He really writes his own songs. He's really sweet and . . ."

"And what?" asked Nat.

Rosalina looked down. "And I really like him."

Nat was devastated.

Nat channeled his anguish as best he knew how. He wrote a new song. He sat at his baby grand piano and played as he sang:

> *My mind turned around.*
> *I'm seeing things upside down.*
> *My mind turned around.*
> *I'm acting like a clown.*
> *'Cause the girl of my dreams was*
> *right next to me and —*
> *She was sitting on my lap.*
> *I didn't catch your name,*
> *but I'm going insane.*

Alex sat on the couch nearby reading a magazine. He tossed his magazine into the air when their dad entered playing his accordion.

"What in the poopoosauce?" asked Alex.

"Hey, guys," said their dad. "I wrote a song for my honey bunny, and later on I'm going over to give her a little serenade."

Alex looked at their dad, wondering what the heck a serenade was.

"What's a serenade?" asked Alex.

"It's when you play a song for someone you really care about. Preferably beneath their window on a moonlit night," explained Mr. Wolff.

"And girls like this serenade stuff?" asked Alex.

"Sure. But it's got to be good." He held up a framed photo of Betty. The platinum blond woman grinned back at them. "That's why I'm practicing in front of her picture. I want to make sure it sounds just right."

Alex walked over to the camera lens and leaned in close. "See this face?" he asked. "This is my, *I'm getting an idea* face."

After making a few phone calls, Alex asked Nat to come with him to their recording studio. Nat didn't know why, but Alex insisted. When they got there, Alex shoved Nat past the sound stages and back to the music studio.

"Why are you taking me here?" asked Nat.

"Just do what I say for once in my eight years on this planet," said Alex.

When they stepped inside, the rest of the band was there and set up. Everyone but Rosalina. Their instruments were plugged in, and microphones pointed at everyone.

"What are you guys doing here?" asked Nat.

"Alex said you wrote a song about Rosalina," replied Qaasim. "We're going to help you record it."

"Then you can lemonade her," said Alex.

"*Lemonade* her?" asked Nat, confused.

"He means *serenade* her," said Thomas. "We'll record the instrumentals, then you play it for her on this boom box and sing to her outside her window." He pointed to the portable stereo on the floor.

"In the moonlight," added David.

"What for?" asked Nat.

"It's romantic," said Qaasim. "And chicks dig romance."

Alex clapped a hand on his shoulder. "Come on, big brother. Go win her back."

With Nat's instructions, the band successfully recorded the new song. And even though they had just learned it, everyone picked it up right away. After a few more tries, they recorded a good take and burned it to a CD.

Soon, Alex and Nat were on their way to Rosalina's

house. Boom box in hand, Nat felt very nervous. Nevertheless, he knew it was the right thing to do.

"Thanks for talking me into this, Alex," said Nat. "I realized I never told Rosalina the way I feel about her. Or that the D flats she plays are cheeky or anything." He nervously fidgeted with his shirt. "I'm going to sing the song and then I'm going to just open up my heart to her." He smiled. "Yeah, this feels really good." He patted Alex on the back. "Thanks again, Alex."

Alex didn't respond. Instead, he pointed to the front of Rosalina's building. Nat looked up and felt as if he'd been hit in the gut. Bobby Love had just then parked his motorcycle and was sauntering up the front steps of Rosalina's brownstone. He rang the doorbell and Rosalina answered. She smiled and let him inside.

Without saying a word, Nat turned and started for home.

Back at their apartment, Nat set the boom box by the front door and shuffled into the living room. He and Alex plopped onto the couch. Nat grabbed the remote and began flipping through the channels. They weren't even bothered by their dad's singing and accordion playing in the background. He practiced a new song he was going to sing with Betty. He sang her parts in a quirky falsetto voice.

My name is Sonny.
My name is Betty.
I think I'm funny.
I like spaghetti.

Their dad stopped playing. "What do you think guys?" he asked. "It's the Honey Bunnies' new duet!"

Nat didn't answer, he stopped channel-surfing when he saw the video of him and the band taken at the photo studio. Nat groaned as the camera zoomed in on him glaring at Bobby Love. The shot switched to reveal Matt

Pinfield. The short, bald man stood in his studio. Pinfield was a TV personality and vocal critic of the Naked Brothers Band.

"I for one think having another band on the bill is a major thumbs-up for the Little Kids Rock charity," said Pinfield. "But not Naked Brother Nat Wolff. Apparently two's a crowd for this rock tot!" He cupped his hands around his mouth. "Yo, Nat. Surf's up! Love is in the air for Rosalina, and it's spelled B-O-B-B-Y. Bobby!"

Alex threw a pillow at the screen. "Actually, it's R-O-B-E-R-T. Robert."

"There's other Nat Wolff news," continued Pinfield. "An inside source told this rock reporter that despite claims to the contrary, Nat Wolff does not write his own songs."

"What?!" asked Nat.

Pinfield's grin widened. "Now if I was a fan of the naked ones, which I assure you, I'm not, I would be outraged at Nat Wolff for taking credit for music that he doesn't write."

This time, Nat threw a pillow. It hit the TV hard enough to switch it off.

The next day, both bands were to meet at the benefit venue — The Turtle Club. They weren't there to rehearse but to hold an official press conference for the event. A podium with a microphone stood in the center of the club's large stage. Several reporters with video cameras were in the audience.

Nat paced while the band waited backstage. He really wasn't in the mood to talk to reporters. He was still fuming over Matt Pinfield's comments. Nat paced faster. He wished Cooper was there. The young manager was much better speaking for them at these kinds of things. Unfortunately, Cooper had a conflicting appointment he couldn't miss.

When the L.A. Surfers arrived, Nat immediately sought out Bobby Love. He cornered him backstage, alone.

"You told Pinfield that lie about me not writing my own songs, didn't you?" asked Nat. "Admit it!"

Bobby gave Nat a look of exaggerated surprise. "Lie? Moi?" He looked up. "Wait, that's French. I'm not French." He dropped the English accent. "Then again, I'm not English either. But you know that. Don't you, little spy?"

Nat got in his face. "I can tell the press that *you're* the liar and the phony. Not me."

Bobby laughed. "No one would believe you, would they, dude? You've already lost your street cred after Matt Pinfield's latest news report." He poked a finger into Nat's chest. "So here's what you're going to do about it —

nothing . . . except watch as I steal your girlfriend *and* your fans."

"She's not my girlfriend," said Nat.

Bobby laughed. "Now who's being a phony?"

As Nat fumed, Patty appeared and stepped between the two boys. "Two minutes!" she announced. "Everybody to the podium!"

Nat was about to walk away when Rosalina joined them. Bobby smiled. "There's the gorgeous Rosalina." His accent returned. "How are you doing today? Reunited with both your earrings?"

"Yes, thanks to you," she said. "That was so sweet of you to drop by yesterday and return them."

"Yeah, sweet," said Nat sarcastically.

Rosalina glared at him. "Yes, sweet!"

Nat reluctantly joined the rest of the Naked Brothers Band on the stage. Soon, Bobby Love joined the L.A. Surfers on the other side. Bobby smiled and waved to the audience.

Patty stepped up to the podium and leaned closer to the microphone. "Hello Big Apple and the world! We're thrilled that this year, not one, but *two* bands are going to help Little Kids Rock! The Naked Brothers Band and the L.A. Surfers!"

Everyone clapped. Then Alex pushed up to the mic. "It's East Coast versus West Coast, baby!"

Patty glanced around nervously. "He's joking! This is not a competition. It's a fund-raiser." She covered the microphone and shook her head. "Rock stars," she muttered. "I told them we should've had a bake sale."

Bobby stepped up and put an arm around Patty. "It's all about the kids."

Patty smiled nervously. "Because Little Kids Rock!"

Nat leaned closer to Bobby but out of the microphone's range. "This isn't about the kids. It's about you being a weasel."

Bobby kept smiling. "And what are you going to do about it, Nate?"

That was all he could stand. "Don't call me Nate!" He reached down and grabbed the back of Bobby Love's underwear. He pulled them up and out, giving him the wedgie of a lifetime.

"Yeah, it's not Nate!" yelled Alex. He stomped one of Bobby's toes. "Mate!"

"You come into my town, crash my charity, and tell lies about me!" yelled Nat.

"Nat, stop!" Rosalina shouted. "You're embarrassing all of us!"

Bobby hopped on one foot. "I don't know what you're talking about." He shoved his underwear back into his pants. "We're here for the kids. We want little kids to rock."

"I'll show you a little kid who rocks and socks!" yelled Alex. He tackled Bobby Love to the ground. That was all the rest of the band needed. Everyone but Rosalina attacked the L.A. Surfers like a pack of wild monkeys. They climbed on their backs, wrestled them to the ground, and poured drinks over their heads.

Nat realized this was wrong. The two bands shouldn't be fighting each other. They were there to help a charity not rumble around like a bunch of kindergarteners. Nat knew he was better than that. The entire Naked Brothers Band was better than that. He felt ashamed for starting the fight in the first place. Luckily, he thought of something that might redeem their honor. It would certainly help the charity and maybe even settle the score with Bobby Love.

He climbed out of the ruckus and grabbed the mic from the podium. "Stop!" he yelled. Feedback echoed from the speakers. "This isn't right. Let's not take this out on each other." Everyone let go of each other and got to their feet.

"Now that's the spirit," said Patty. She stepped back behind the podium.

Nat turned to the reporters. "Let's take this out onstage! This weekend at the concert!"

"What?" asked Patty. "No!"

Nat pointed at Bobby Love. "The Naked Brothers Band challenge the L.A. Surfers to a battle of the bands!" He turned back to Patty. "The loser donates all the money from the next CD to Little Kids Rock."

She beamed. "On the other hand . . . woo-hoo!"

Nat addressed the reporters. "And I want all our fans out there to know that I do write my own songs! And we're going to play a new song at the concert!"

Bobby Love staggered forward and snatched the mic from Nat's hand. "If that's what's best for the charity, we accept your challenge." It was his turn to address the cameras. "And to all *our* fans out there, I want you to know that the L.A. Surfers will play a new song, too!" He turned back to Nat. "May the best band win."

Nat's eyes narrowed. "Oh, we will."

9

The next day, the Naked Brothers Band was back at the club for yet another press conference. Cooper had insisted on it. The entire band sat at a long table on the stage. Nat rubbed his temples, trying to hide his face. He was very embarrassed.

When all of the reporters had assembled, Cooper leaned forward and spoke into the microphone. He read from a prepared statement. "The Naked Brothers Band would like to extend their apologies to the L.A. Surfers for any injuries they might have received in yesterday's altercation at the Little Kids Rock press conference. I would like to apologize on my own behalf because my mom scheduled an orthodontist appointment for me, which conflicted with the conference, so I was unable to be there. I feel if I had been, I might have been able to help smooth over this situation before it got out of hand." He glared at Nat then went back to his speech. "We wish the very best to the L.A. Surfers and look forward to our friendly competition with them Saturday at this wonderful charity event. Thank you. No further questions."

Everyone stood and headed off the stage. Rosalina strode next to Cooper. "That was great. Thanks for doing that."

"No problem," said Cooper. "It's all part of my job."

Thomas sneered. "I didn't hear the L.A. Surfers calling a press conference to apologize to us. Did you, David?"

"No, I didn't, Thomas," he turned to Qaasim. "Did you, Qaasim?"

"No I didn't, David," said Qaasim. "Did you, Alex?"

"No I didn't, Qaasim," said Alex. He turned to Nat. "Did you, Nat?"

"No I didn't, Alex." He glared at Rosalina. "Did you?"

"No I didn't, Nat." She glared back. "Because the L.A. Surfers had nothing to apologize for." She pushed past the others and stormed out the stage door.

Thomas leaned close to David. "We told Nat it was a bad idea to put a girl in the band," he whispered.

"You're right," said David. "He can't say we didn't warn him."

"'Boys Rule, Girls Drool' was the best song I ever wrote," said Thomas.

David gave him a high five. "I don't know why that song wasn't a hit."

"Different times, my friend," said Thomas. "Different times."

"You think?" asked David.

"Oh yeah," replied Thomas. "The world wasn't ready for it. People liked girls better back then."

"Ahh," said David. He followed the others outside.

Back at the apartment, Nat sat in the polka-dot room with his dad and Alex. One of the great things about being a rock star is that they got to decorate their homes any way they wanted. The unusual room was painted with huge red polka dots. Round windows and a bench seat lined the circular wall. The bench and floor were covered in yellow shag carpeting. That wasn't the oddest thing in the room though. The oddest thing was the three of them sitting there, wearing basketball hoop hats. Netted hoops covered their heads like large, orange halos.

"Guys, you might have wondered why I called this head basketball meeting," said their dad.

Nat sighed. "Yeah, dad, we're not really in the mood."

"I understand," said Mr. Wolff. "You boys have a lot on your mind right now. But . . . well . . ." He looked anxious.

"Betty and I have been doing a lot of practicing these past few days, and we were wondering if we could be your opening act for the Battle of the Bands on Saturday."

Alex rolled his eyes. "Here we go."

Nat and Alex's father was always trying to get in on the act. He was a great guy and the best dad in the world. But the Naked Brothers Band really didn't have room for an accordion.

"You and Betty?" asked Nat.

"Yes," he replied. "Betty and me."

"You and Betty have a band?" asked Nat.

Their dad's eyes widened. "Oh yes. Didn't I tell you? We have our own little band now. The Honey Bunnies."

"Oh, boy," said Alex. He began to toss some foam basketballs into Nat's hat.

"Dad, putting other bands on the bill . . ." Nat glanced at Alex. "It's not up to us."

"Yes it is," said Alex. "And we say no way, José. With a capital H!"

"I understand, I understand," said their Dad. "I just thought with all your wherewithal and what not, you could . . ."

Nat put a hand on his dad's shoulder. "We'll see what we can do."

"We will?" asked Alex.

"Yeah," he replied. "What have we got to lose? It's all a big mess anyway." Besides, he hated turning his dad down *all* the time.

"Right!" said their dad. "It's all a big mess anyway! What have you got to lose?"

Alex shook Nat by the shoulders. "Nat, you don't know what you're saying. It's the heartbreak talking!"

Nat laughed and pushed his hands away. "Yes, I do. And I know the day is already ruined for our band. So someone in our family might as well be happy. And if the L.A. Surfers can share the stage with the Naked Brothers Band, why can't the Honey Bunnies?"

Their dad leaped to his feet. He began hopping up and down. "Why can't the Honey Bunnies?! Why can't the Honey Bunnies?!" Foam basketballs spilled from his hoop hat.

"Well, when you put it that way . . ." said Alex.

"So you'll do it?" their dad asked. "You'll put the Honey Bunnies on the bill?"

"We'll try," Nat replied. "But don't get your hopes up."

"Yeah," agreed Alex. "We really upset that Little

Kids Rock girl. She might not want to do us any favors right now."

"True. It had better not come from us," said Nat.

Cooper walked through the offices of the Little Kids Rock Foundation. He passed several cubicles, stacks of donated instruments, and a huge crate full of harmonicas. He reached up and adjusted the orthodontic headgear that encircled his head. His mouth was sore, and he really didn't feel up to negotiating today, but a manager's job is never finished. He marched straight to Patty Scoggins's office. He knocked on the open door and stepped inside. Patty sat behind a desk covered in stacks of paper.

"First, I'd like to introduce myself." He extended his hand over the desk. "I'm Cooper Pillot. I manage the Naked Brothers Band."

"I know who you are," said Patty. She glowered at him and crossed her arms. "You should be ashamed of yourself, going to an orthodontist appointment and leaving me to deal with your band of wild animals."

"I'm sorry. I had to go. I needed to be fitted for my headgear," said Cooper. He touched the metal wires that surrounded his head.

"Get your priorities straight, Mr. Pillot." She pointed to her own orthodontic device. "My headgear never interfered with my work. The fight the Naked Brothers Band started gave our charity some very bad publicity."

Cooper sat in one of the guest chairs. "Well, it's a matter of opinion who started the fight, Miss . . ."

"Scoggins," she said. "And no, it is not a matter of opinion. It is a matter of fact that Nat Wolff bullied that poor, sweet Bobby Love."

It was time for Cooper to pour on the charm. "I understand that you feel that way, Miss Scoggins, and I'm prepared to make it up to you."

She looked at him suspiciously "How?"

"Have you heard of the Honey Bunnies?"

"No," she replied. "Who are the Honey Bunnies?"

"Only a band so huge in Europe that you can't go anywhere without hearing their music on the radio," he replied.

"If they're so big, why haven't we heard of them in America?" asked Patty.

Cooper shook his head. "The Honey Bunnies won't release any CDs in the States because they want to maintain their European mystique." He raised a finger. "However, I pulled some strings and they are willing to play for your charity because they admire Little Kids Rock and all the good work you've been doing."

Her eyes widened. "They've heard about us in Europe?"

"Oh yes, Miss Scoggins," replied Cooper.

"And we'd have an exclusive on premiering the Honey Bunnies?" asked Patty.

"Oh yeah." Cooper grinned. "The Honey Bunnies would be all yours."

10

Ever since the press conference, Bobby Love had been racking his brain trying to come up with a new song. He stayed up all night but he couldn't come up with anything. Finally, like the appearance of a giant wave, it suddenly appeared. Bobby realized that he should write about the greatest love of his life. He couldn't believe he didn't think of it before.

The L.A. Surfers had set up their instruments in one of the club's dressing rooms. Bobby handed out the lead sheets to the other band members and instructed them how to play. As they began the intro, Bobby cleared his throat. It was time to unveil his masterpiece.

I slick you back,
I spike you up,
You never let me down.
And when the morning comes,
I treat you nice,
Never forgetting to wash you twice.

Wash, rinse, repeat.
That is the story of our love.
Wash, rinse, repeat

Randy stopped playing guitar. He held up his hands until the entire band quit playing. When it was quiet, he turned to Bobby. "Dude, we can't sing that song."

"Why not, dude?" asked Bobby. He didn't have to use his English accent in front of his bandmates. He spoke in his usual surfer drawl.

Jeff twirled a drumstick. "It reeks, dude."

"Dude, they'd laugh us off the stage," said Randy.

"Why?" asked Bobby. He ran a comb through his hair. "Everybody loves my hair, dude."

"Not as much as you might think, dude," said Jeff.

Pork raised a hand. "I love it."

Bobby pointed his comb at Pork. "Pork loves it." Pork wasn't the brightest bulb in the box, but Bobby would take any support he got.

Pork chuckled. "I think I'm losing a little hair, man." He ran a hand through his greasy hair. "I love hair. I treasure hair. Bobby's got so much hair. I love your hair, Bobby. I do."

Bobby laughed nervously. "See, everybody loves my hair."

Randy set down his guitar. "Dude, we're *not* singing about your hair."

"Yeah. It's really embarrassing," Jeff added. "Just have Bernie write a new song as usual."

Bobby cringed. "Uh, Bernie quit."

"Bernie quit?!" asked Randy.

"Yeah I was just messing with his head, dude," Bobby explained. "And I said he was fired and he quit! Dude, do you believe that?"

"Dude, what are we going to do?" asked Jeff.

"Let's sing the hair song," said Pork.

Randy raised his hands. "The hair song is voted down, Pork."

Bobby Love plopped into his chair. "We've got to get another song by tomorrow or the Naked Brothers Band is going to kick our butts."

11

The Naked Brothers Band had their equipment set up in the dressing room on the other side of the stage. They each played their instruments as they rehearsed Nat's new song. As usual, Ken and Mohammed videotaped their performance. Cooper tapped a foot to the beat as Nat sang.

L.A. L.A. L.A. L.A. go today.
L.A. L.A. L.A. L.A. it's a date.

Nat smiled and glanced at Rosalina. He added an extra lyric.

Bobby Love is a big fat, phony liar.

Everyone laughed but Rosalina. "Okay, if you guys won't rehearse the song with the right lyrics, I'm leaving," she said.

"Go ahead and leave," said Thomas.

"Go join Bobby Love's band across the way, since you love him so much," taunted Alex.

"Maybe I should," barked Rosalina.

Cooper raised his hands. "You guys, stop it right now. Just rehearse the song the way Nat wrote it. Originally, I mean."

They played the intro again then Nat sang.

L.A. L.A. L.A. L.A. go today.

L.A. L.A. L.A. L.A. it's a date.

Nat couldn't resist.

Bobby Love is a big fat, phony liar.

Once again, everyone but Cooper and Rosalina burst into laughter. "Nat, stop it right now!" Cooper ordered.

Rosalina unplugged her bass guitar. "I quit!"

Nat stopped laughing. "What?"

"I think you guys are acting mean!" yelled Rosalina. She packed away her sheet music and her guitar. "And I don't like being ganged up on just because I don't hate someone you hate." She zipped up her guitar case and slung it over her shoulder. She glared at Thomas and David. "I knew you guys could be jerks sometimes." She rounded on Nat. "But I expected more from you. Good-bye." She pushed through the dressing room door.

Bobby Love left his dressing room in time to see Rosalina cross the stage. She put down her gear and sat on a crate in the middle of the stage. Never missing an opportunity to stick it to Nat, Bobby sat beside her and asked her what was wrong. She told him how she had quit the band.

"I don't know what to do. I didn't even want to quit," said Rosalina. "I'm not a quitting kind of person. I just hated the way they all talked about you. Especially Nat."

"Jealousy is a destructive emotion, Rosalina," said Bobby in his English accent. "Have you ever noticed that the word *lousy* is in the word jealousy?"

Rosalina gave him a confused look. "Yeah . . ."

"That's because jealousy makes you feel lousy," he continued.

"Right," she said. "You said that to me the other day, remember?"

Bobby nodded his head. "It bears repeating."

"Yeah, I guess it does," said Rosalina. She sighed. "Nat keeps saying you're a phony. Your accent, your songwriting, the way you feel about this children's charity . . ."

"The children are our future, Rosalina," said Bobby.

"Right. You said that to me too. Remember?" asked Rosalina.

"It bears repeating," Bobby repeated. He made a mental note: Come up with some new lines.

Rosalina grimaced. "You didn't tell Matt Pinfield lies about Nat not writing his songs, did you?" she asked.

Bobby took her hands in his and put on his serious face. "Rosalina, look into my eyes. Do I look like a liar to you?"

She smiled. "No. It's just . . . well, do you write your songs?"

"Of course I do," he replied. He pretended to be outraged. "Who said I didn't?"

"Nat did," she replied. "So, where in England are you from?"

"Where in England?" he repeated the question. He had to think of something. He didn't know anything about England. Then he noticed a page of sheet music poking out of the pocket of her guitar case. "Is that your music?"

Rosalina glanced down. "Yeah. I guess I won't be needing it now that I quit the band."

Bobby snatched up the page and ceremoniously crumpled it into a ball. He tossed it into a nearby trash can. "There you are. Quick and easy does the trick. It's less painful that way."

She tried to smile, but looked like she was about to cry. "I don't know. Is it? I'm not sure."

"Oh, trust me," said Bobby. "I've been through this kind of thing. Just throw your music away and move on."

Bobby put an arm around her, as if trying to comfort her. He drew her close and turned up the charm. "A beautiful girl like you has a lot of beautiful music ahead of her."

Rosalina pulled away from him. "Do you mind if we . . ." she stood and grabbed her case. "Right now, I'm a little . . . confused." She turned and ran away. "I'm sorry."

Bobby Love wasn't sorry to see her go. In fact, he thought she would never leave. He hopped up and reached into the trash can. He pulled out the sheet music and smoothed it out. "Perfect," he said with a smile.

The night of the big concert, Cooper escorted the band (all but Rosalina) to their dressing room. Everyone was dressed up and ready for the show. Cooper left the band to rehearse in their dressing room. He crossed the stage and noticed that it was all set up for the show. Large amplifiers were stacked in front of draping, red velvet curtains. A large video screen hung above them.

Cooper hopped off the stage and found Patty Scoggins sitting in the empty seating area. He sat down beside her.

"Mr. Pillot, I tested the video you gave me to project behind the Naked Brother's song 'L.A.'" She held up a videotape. "And it's not what you told me it would be."

"It's not images of Los Angeles?" asked Cooper.

"No," she replied. "It's just documentary footage of your band singing the song."

"Oh, I must have gotten the tapes mixed up." Cooper reached into his pocket and pulled out his backup copy. A good manager always carried backups. "Here you go." He traded tapes with her. "Thank you for catching the mistake, Miss Scoggins."

Just then, Mr. Wolff and his girlfriend, Betty, stepped onto the stage. Betty wore a bright pink outfit while Mr. Wolff wore a powder blue one. She carried a ukulele while Mr. Wolff held his accordion. They both wore large bunny ears on their heads. Cooper cringed.

Patty pointed to the stage. "Who are they?"

"Those are the Honey Bunnies," he replied. "They're doing their sound check."

Patty's eyes widened. "*Those* are the Honey Bunnies?"

"Yep," said Cooper.

"From Europe?" asked Patty.

"Yep," he repeated.

Patty frowned "But, they're so . . . old."

"Europe is a very old continent," said Cooper.

Her face softened. "True."

The Honey Bunnies began to sing and play. Cooper winced and reached into his coat-pocket. He pulled out two small packages. He offered one to Patty. "Earplugs?"

She snatched them up. "Thank you, Mr. Pillot."

Back in their dressing room, Nat and the band finished their final rehearsal. They sounded great (except for the fact that they didn't have a bass player). Nat wondered if Rosalina would even show up for the concert tonight. He wished he could apologize to her. He didn't even want to convince her that Bobby Love was faking. He just wanted her back in the band and back in his life.

The dressing room door flew open. Unfortunately, it wasn't Rosalina. It was his dad and Betty. "Yoo-hoo, boys," said Betty. "Did you hear our sound check?"

Unlucky for them, they did. A video feed was piped into the dressing room and played on the TV monitor.

"Yup," said Alex. "We heard it." He leaned close to Nat. "They have Honey Bunny costumes?" he whispered.

"Yeah," Nat replied.

"Yuck," said Alex.

"Well, we better practice some more," said their dad. He and Betty giggled with excitement as they shuffled out of the room.

"They're really in love," said Nat.

"We don't need Rosalina, Nat," said Thomas.

"Yeah," agreed David. "You have to get your spirits up, so we can kick their surfer butts."

Nat sighed. "What does it matter if we win or lose? Rosalina will still hate me and love Bobby Love."

From their dressing room, Nat could hear the rumble of the crowd as they slowly filled the club. Once the seats were full, they were only minutes from show time. From the room's monitor, he could see the house lights darken. Nat didn't feel up to the show, but he was going to try his best for the charity. Unfortunately, to make matters worse, Matt Pinfield was at the club. Nat watched the monitors as he conducted pre-show interviews.

Matt Pinfield stepped onto the stage. "It's time to rock, America!" he yelled. The audience cheered him with equal enthusiasm. "This is it. We're live and on the Internet, coming into your home for the Little Kids Rock benefit in New York City!" He gave his devious grin. "Tonight, we separate the boys . . . or should I say the Surfers from the Brothers in a winner-take-all Battle of the Bands contest!" The crowd cheered louder.

Pinfield stepped to the side as Bobby Love joined him on the stage. "Bobby, who's going to win tonight?"

"The real winners are going to be the kids, Matt," replied Bobby. "As you know, the losing band is going to donate all the proceeds of their next CD to Little Kids Rock."

"What about your new song?" asked Pinfield. "Is it a winner?"

Bobby smiled into the camera. "I didn't come here to lose."

A little girl appeared at the bottom of the screen. She approached the stage holding a pink balloon on a string. "Here, Bobby." She held out the balloon. "I brought you a balloon for luck."

Bobby's eyes widened. He took a step back. "Uh . . . I have to go get ready."

Nat laughed. *What a wimp.*

Alex stepped onto the stage. He had agreed to take Nat's place for the pre-show interview. The girl offered him the balloon. "Here Alex, you can have my balloon," she said. She looked back at the camera. "I hope your band kicks Bobby's band's booty!"

Alex smiled and took the balloon. "Thanks."

"Hey, where's Nat?" asked Pinfield. "I wanted to inter-view him."

"Tough patootie," said Alex. "You got me, baldy."

Pinfield sneered. "Is Nat busy crying over his girl-friend leaving the band?"

Maybe Matt Pinfield is the real wimp, Nat thought.

"No," said Alex. He poked the man in the chest. "He's busy getting ready to kick Bobby's band's booty!" He gave the girl a thumbs-up and walked away with the balloon.

Nat stood and put on his jacket. Alex might be a pain sometimes, but he was the best little brother in the world.

As Nat left the dressing room, Bobby Love was standing there waiting for him. "Hello, mate. Looking forward to getting snookered by the L.A. Surfers tonight?"

"Aren't you supposed to be on your side of the stage?" asked Nat.

"Yeah, but I missed my old mate, Nat," Bobby replied.

Nat glared up at him. "You don't have to be English around me, remember?"

Bobby glanced around. "Can't be too safe, mate. The walls have ears. And so do all those documentary cameras of yours. I'm sure there's one around here somewhere spying on us. I know how much you love to spy."

Anger boiled inside Nat. He wanted to fling himself at the faker but he knew better. He was here to put on a show and that was it. He began to walk back into his dressing room.

"Heartbroken to hear about your bass player quitting, by the way," Bobby shouted after him. "Bad luck, right? You'll be glad to know I comforted her in her hour of need."

That was it. Nat spun around and leaped for Bobby Love. He tackled him around the waist, but the older boy was ready for him this time. He easily pushed Nat to the ground. Nat struggled to break free, but Bobby just laughed.

Then Alex appeared beside them. He still held the pink balloon on the string. Bobby sprung off Nat and backed away. "Get that thing away from me!" His accent vanished, and terror appeared in his eyes.

Alex moved closer to him. "Stay away from my brother, balloon wimp!"

"Okay, okay," agreed Bobby. "Just don't let go of the string, please, dude!" He stumbled and ran off.

Alex helped Nat to his feet. "I wouldn't have believed it if I hadn't seen it with my own eyes," said Alex.

"I hear you, man," said Nat.

It was finally time for the show to begin. Nat waited in the wings with the rest of his band and the Honey Bunnies. Luckily, the L.A. Surfers were still in their dressing room. Just before the show began, Nat spotted Rosalina standing on the other side of the stage. Their eyes met briefly, then she looked away. Nat tried not to think about her. He just had to perform his song, and then he could go home and sulk all he wanted. Until then, the charity needed him.

The lights dimmed and Patty walked onto the stage. A spotlight circled her as she stepped toward the microphone stand. A younger kid followed her. He wore glasses and a sweater vest. He held a shiny new harmonica. The audience applauded as she grabbed the mic.

"Welcome to the Little Kids Rock Battle of the Bands Benefit!" she said. "Tonight we can use the power of music to put music in the hands of our greatest resource — kids." She gestured to the boy beside her.

He looked down at his harmonica then back to Patty. "I wanted a tuba."

"Well, you got a harmonica," Patty said through clenched teeth. The boy hung his head and walked offstage.

Patty turned back to the audience. "And now, all the way from old Europe, please welcome the Honey Bunnies!"

The club roared as Mr. Wolff and Betty shuffled onto the stage. After the crowd got a good look at them, the cheering died down. Mr. Wolff beamed as he began to play his accordion. Betty quickly joined in on her ukulele. That wasn't the worst of it; they then began to sing.

My name is Sonny.
My name is Betty.
I think I'm funny.
I like spaghetti.

The crowd booed loudly but the Honey Bunnies kept singing happily.

Patty turned to Cooper. "This isn't going to make little kids rock. This is going to make them want to give up music forever."

"What can I tell you?" asked Cooper. "They're big in Europe."

The little kid shoved the harmonica into Patty's hand. "Take it. I'm through with music." He stormed away.

Patty chased after him. "I can get you a tuba!"

Nat stared at his father and Betty as they sang. They smiled and gazed into one another's eyes as if they were the only ones around. "Dad's so lucky," said Nat.

Alex covered his ears. "Are you crazy? He's getting booed off the stage."

"Who cares?" asked Nat. "She loves him."

Back in their dressing room, the L.A. Surfers finished rehearsing Nat's song. Bobby was surprised at how good they sounded with only a couple of rehearsals. *That Nat Wolff was a pretty good songwriter after all*, he thought.

"This is really a great song, Bobby," said Randy. "When did you have time to write this?"

"Yeah, Bobby, I'm impressed," Jeff added. "I didn't know you could write a song this good."

"See, dudes, you doubted me." He cocked his head. "But who loves you?"

They chanted in unison. "Bobby Love loves us!"

Bobby put a hand to one ear. "I can't hear you."

"Bobby Love loves us!" they yelled.

"That's right," Bobby said with a smile. He looked up at the monitor. The Honey Bunnies still sang amid the barrage of boos. "We're up next after these losers," he said. "And if the Naked Brothers drop out, the Honey Bunnies will be our only competition."

"Why would they drop out?" asked Randy.

"Trust me," assured Bobby. "We'll be a hard act for them to follow."

Nat stepped aside as his dad and Betty shuffled off the stage. They were both beaming with joy. The audience continued to boo behind them.

"Are they saying *woo woo*?" asked Betty.

"Yeah," said Mr. Wolff. "I think we knocked them dead!"

Betty jumped up and down. "Woo! Woo!"

Nat saw the L.A. Surfers pile out of their dressing room. They looked confident and psyched. Bobby Love caught Nat's eye and grinned. Nat rolled his eyes and looked away.

Patty ran back to the stage and raised her hands. The rowdy crowd fell silent. "Next up, the band that likes to hang ten in the top ten," she said. "Let's hear the love for the L.A. Surfers!"

The crowd roared as the band ran onto the stage. Bobby cradled the mic stand in his hands. "Thank you!" he yelled over the cheers. "The Surfers and I are truly chuffed to be here tonight, rockin' out for all the kids out there who can't. We hope this song makes a difference. It's a ditty I wrote about a city I call home!"

Nat got a bad feeling about this.

Bobby leaped into the air, and the electric guitar wailed. The bass drum rumbled the floor, and the bass guitar thumped along to the beat. Bobby danced around during the song's intro, and the girls in the audience squealed. When he made his way back to the mic, very familiar words left his mouth.

The time in our favorite place is going too fast
The time we spent here is already in the past
L.A., L.A., L.A., L.A., go today
L.A., L.A., L.A., L.A., it's a date
L.A., L.A., L.A., L.A., say hoorah

Nat gaped in disbelief. The rest of the band did the same.

"Holy moley on a cracker," said Alex.

"That's . . . that's our song," said Nat.

"They stole our song!" shouted Qaasim.

"That's your song?" asked Patty.

"It sure is," said Cooper.

"Rosalina must have given it to them," said Thomas.

"She never would have done that," said Nat.

Qaasim shook his head. "Man, that's the love talking."

Rosalina ran behind the back curtain and joined them. "He stole my music!" she shouted. Her eyes welled with tears. "You guys, I'm so sorry. Nat, I'm so, so sorry! I can't believe this is happening."

"It's okay," said Nat. "It's okay."

"No, it's not," said Rosalina.

"No, it's not," Alex agreed.

Rosalina shook her head. "I'm such an idiot."

Nat put a hand on her shoulder. "No, you're not."

"Yes, she is," said Alex.

"Shut up, Alex," he snapped. "She feels bad enough as it is."

"So he is a liar and a phony after all," said Patty. She turned to Cooper. "Do you still have the tape? The one that had your band playing this same song?"

"Yeah," said Cooper. He dug it out of his jacket.

Patty held out a hand. "Give it to me. I have an idea."

Cooper gave her the tape and she ran off.

Rosalina sat on a crate and buried her face in her hands. "It's horrible to realize that everything you admire about someone is a lie." She glanced up. "I wish those balloons were made of cement and they'd all fall on Bobby Love's big, fat, phony head!"

Balloons? Nat looked up. A huge net full of balloons drooped over the stage. They must have planned to drop them as part of the grand finale. Nat pointed to them. "Guys! Balloons!"

"Right," said Thomas. "He's afraid of balloons!"

Rosalina looked up. "You mean he really is afraid of balloons?" She looked at Bobby Love with disgust. "What a wimp."

Alex dug through a draped curtain and found a thin white cord. He held it out. "Let's pull the ripcord on those things."

Nat took the cord and offered it to Rosalina. "Would you like to do the honors?"

She took the thin rope and smiled. "Thank you."

Rosalina pulled the cord, and a seam opened in the center of the net. Balloons of every color drifted down on the L.A. Surfers. The rest of the band didn't seem to notice. Bobby Love, on the other hand, promptly freaked out.

"Dude! Balloons! Run for your life!" he yelled. His English accent was gone as he yelped and swatted them away. "Help! Balloons! Mommy! Balloons are like so scary, man! Get them away from me! Help! Somebody save me!" He tried to run off the stage but he was surrounded. "Red ones! Oh no! I hate the red ones most! They're touching my feet!" He shrieked once more, then ran screaming through the mass of balloons.

The band quit playing, and the music faded away. With the music gone, Nat could hear the audience roaring with laughter.

Patty returned and stood next to Cooper. "This should do the trick," she said.

A video image appeared on the screen behind the L.A. Surfers. The scene showed the Naked Brothers Band rehearsing Nat's song "L.A." back on the sound stage.

"Miss Scoggins, you're awesome," said Cooper.

"Call me Patty," she said.

The audience fell quiet as the video played. On the stage, Randy turned to the others. "Hey, that's Bobby's new song."

"How come they know Bobby's new song?" asked Pork.

Suddenly the audience was alive with sound once more. However, this time they booed the L.A. Surfers off the stage.

As the band members ran out in shame, Matt Pinfield ran on. He grabbed the mic. "In a shocking turn of events, it has been revealed that Bobby Love's supposedly 'brand-new song' was stolen from none other than the Naked Brothers Band."

Good, thought Nat. It was about time Matt Pinfield put his big mouth to some good for a change.

And if that isn't enough to shock you," Pinfield continued. "We have also made the discovery that Bobby Love has been faking an English accent all along. He's really balloon-fearing surfer dude, Robert Love from California." He chuckled. "I repeat, Bobby Love is afraid of balloons and is from San Diego." He took the mic from the stand and moved closer to the audience. "Bobby is a thief!" he chanted. "Bobby is a thief!" The audience chanted with him.

16

In their dressing room, the L.A. Surfers packed up their gear as quickly as possible. From the sound of the crowd, they would probably have to slip out the back door. Hopefully, they could get out before anyone knew they were gone.

"I can't believe you stole their song," said Jeff.

Randy zipped up his guitar case. "Dude, I can't believe you're scared of balloons."

Pork held up a small harmonica. "I can't believe they let us keep these cool harmonicas!" He gave it a blow.

Bobby slumped in his chair. "I can't believe we have to donate all of our money from the next CD to this stupid charity."

"Don't worry," said Randy. "After your perfor- mance tonight, there won't be a next CD." He slung his case over his shoulder and grabbed Bobby Love by the leather jacket. He pulled him along as the group slinked out of the dressing room.

As Matt Pinfield worked the audience into a frenzy, Nat went over his new song with Rosalina. Since the Surfers had cribbed their song, they would have to sing his newest new song, 'Girl of My Dreams.' Lucky for them, the rest of the band already knew it since they helped him make the serenade CD. They were also lucky that Rosalina had brought her bass guitar and was an extremely talented musician.

"It's B flat, F over A, and G minor." He pointed to the sheet music. "Then sing *aaaaah*, for the backup right here."

"Got it," she said.

Nat gave her a smile. "Welcome back."

Meanwhile, Patty had ushered Matt Pinfield off the stage. She tried desperately to quiet the audience before they turned into a lynch mob.

"Ladies and gentlemen, please settle down," she said. The audience kept chanting and yelling. Patty turned to Nat. "Please save me, Naked Brothers Band."

"Let's go," said Nat. He led the way as they took the stage.

The audience stopped chanting and erupted into cheers. Patty handed the mic to Nat as the others set up their equipment. Nat raised a hand, and the audience's roar faded to silence. "Let's hear it for the Honey Bunnies and the L.A. Surfers who did a great cover of our new song, 'L.A.'" The audience rumbled, but Nat didn't give them a chance to get rowdy again. "Unfortunately that was the song we had planned to sing for you this evening. So, if we make a few mistakes on the one we play now, try to understand. Because this is an even newer song." The crowd cheered. When they settled, Nat continued. "I wrote this for a person who is very special to me," he glanced at Rosalina. She smiled back. "I was actually in a lot of pain when I wrote it," he continued. "But I'm really happy now. And for the first time I can actually enjoy singing it. It's called 'Girl of My Dreams.'"

Alex slapped his drumsticks together, counting down. On the fifth beat, he slammed them onto the drum heads. Qaasim wailed on the guitar as Nat and David played the keyboards. Thomas ran his bow across his cello strings, and Rosalina tapped her foot as she thumbed at her bass strings. Nat leaned closer to the mic.

My mind turned around
I'm seeing things upside down
My mind turned around

I'm acting like a clown
The girl of my dreams
Was right next to me
And she was sitting on my lap

The audience smiled and swayed with the music. Nat had been in front of a lot of audiences before and had learned to read them. He could tell that this audience liked their new song. He glanced over at Rosalina. She smiled back at him. He could tell she liked it too.

Ah ah ah
Ah ah ah ah ah
What if the girl
Of my dreams
Was right next to me?

As they sang the chorus, Rosalina moved closer and shared the mic with Nat. She sang the *ah*'s and hit every note perfectly. In fact, the Naked Brothers Band was back together and played better than ever. And, as it turned out, the girl of his dreams *was* right next to him.

Ah ah ah
Ah ah ah ah ah
What if the girl
Of my dreams
Was right next to me?

OK, so maybe the crazy life is not exactly my style. Or, as Rosalina so nicely put it I'm "so *not* bad to the bone." I guess she's right. But don't you ever feel like maybe if you were someone else, things would be easier?

It all started when we agreed to do the Little Kids Rock charity concert. We were going to play with the L.A. Surfers, a band that the ladies l-o-v-e, thanks to their lead-singer Bobby Love. He's like this punk guy with a British accent. You know the type, wears leather, has piercings, rides a motorcycle. So when I found out that Rosalina was totally crushing on him, I felt like the regular old Nat Wolff just wasn't interesting enough. How could I compete with a guy who can play guitar, surf, and drink coffee all at once?

I was going to play it cool and try to befriend him until Alex and I accidentally ended up spying on him. (I swear! It was an accident!) We were in the bathroom washing the orange out of my hair (which I'd put in there to impress Rosalina, who totally laughed in my face) when we heard someone coming. So we hid in a stall, and in walks Bobby Love and Pork, this other guy in his band (who btw must have the IQ of a peanut). So we're hiding, and Bobby Love totally confessed everything. He wasn't from England, he didn't write his own songs, and he was going to try and flirt with Rosalina.

Whoa. This was more information than we were expecting to get hiding in a toilet stall. We had the whole confession on tape too! (Thanks, Ken!) But, when I tried to tell Rosalina about what I heard she totally didn't believe me.

Meanwhile good old Bobby Love was using his faux-British charms to woo Rosalina. You know, telling her things like her C7 chords sound "cheeky" and returning her earrings late at night.

I think Qaasim said it best: "It's a proven fact. Girls always fall for phonies." And unfortunately, Rosalina was no exception to that. She fell for Bobby Love, hook, line, and sinker. And the more I tried to convince her that he was no good, the more she hated me and the harder she fell for him.

It got so bad, that she actually quit the band. That was the worst. Double whammy: I lost Rosalina, and the band lost its bassist. Talk about a bad day.

But the worst was yet to come. At the Battle of the Bands, when the L.A. Surfers started to play, their song sounded familiar...REALLY familiar. That wanna-be Brit had totally stolen our song!

Luckily, that made Rosalina realize just what a phony Bobby Love
really was.

Then I remembered something that
Jesse had told us: Bobby Love is terri-
fied of balloons (totally random, but
what a wimp!). So Rosalina and I pulled
this ripcord backstage in the middle
of the Surfers' set, and all these
balloons poured down on them. Bobby
totally FLIPPED OUT. Not so much the
charming gent anymore, old chap, are
ya? Ha ha!

After the band was exposed as a
bunch of fakes, we took the stage and
played a new song I wrote for Rosalina
called "Girl of My Dreams." Even though
we didn't have it down all the way
because it was still so new, it sounded
great. And best of all, I think Rosalina
liked it a lot.

So, I guess the story has a happy
ending, and next time, I know that I
don't need to try to be anyone else. So

what if I'm not living la vida loca?
Things are crazy enough as it is!

All right, gotta go shoot some hoops
with Alex. Catch you later.

- Nat

I always try to see the best in people.
You know, I try to be open-minded and
accepting. I think that most people are
good deep down inside. But sometimes,
people are just low-down, dirty, and
good for nothing.

And if you talked to me a day ago,
I would never have put Bobby Love into
that category, but today, I know the
truth: Bobby Love is the worst of
the worst. OK, I know that sounds harsh,
but seriously – he completely tried to
sabotage the Naked Brothers Band.

All right. I admit it. I used
to have the BIGGEST crush EVER on Bobby
Love. I thought he was so dreamy. Those
eyes, that hair, and the leather jacket.

I mean, I really liked his music, too. And he has really good handwriting. I even had his picture up as the screensaver on my computer. (Oh, but I'm sure you already knew that because David and Thomas love to snoop and can't keep their big mouths shut about anything.)

So when I found out that we were going to do a charity event with Bobby's band, the L.A. Surfers, I was so excited! But I guess I was the only one in the band who was happy about it. Everyone else seemed to have a huge problem with Bobby Love. I knew they were all just jealous, but I thought Nat was better than that.

After the charity event, the band totally attacked Bobby Love and the L.A. Surfers for no reason. They had a huge fight, and I was so embarrassed to be a part of the Naked Brothers Band. I mean, we were seriously laughing stocks of the music world. The incident was so bad that Cooper called a press

conference the next day to issue a pub-
lic statement of apology.

The next day at practice when the
teasing began again, I just lost it.
Right there and then, I quit the band.
I thought I was doing the right thing,
but I was really upset afterward. Bobby
convinced me that the best way to get
over it was to start fresh, which meant
throwing away my music to the song we
were going to perform at the Battle of
the Bands. I was so naïve that I actually listened to him, but little did I
know that as soon as I left the room, he
was going to steal the sheet music out
of the trash!

So when the time came for the L.A.
Surfers to perform at the Battle, guess
what song they were playing? Nat's song!
I felt like such an idiot. Bobby Love
really was a fake!

Nat and I wanted revenge...and
it turns out, Bobby Love is totally
balloon-a-phobic. So when we dropped a

whole ton of them on him and his band
while they were playing, he went
bonkers.

It was so funny! Then Nat taught me
this new song called "Girl of My Dreams,"
and I got to play onstage with the band
again. It was great.

Phew, a crazy couple of days for
sure. But everything's back to normal
now. Thank goodness! ;)

OK, time to go practice. Love you
all so much! Keep checking out our
tunes!

xo
- Rosalina

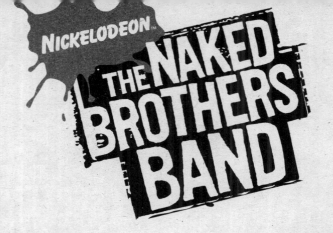

ROCK 'N' READ!

Can't get enough of the Naked Brothers Band? Well, then check out all these new books. Get ready. Get set. Get rockin'!

0-545-02071-9 The Making of the Naked Brothers Band Scrapbook
Get the scoop on the Naked Brothers Band with this scrapbook featuring lots of photos and tons of behind the scenes info!

0-545-02072-7 The Naked Brothers Band Poster Song Book
Learn the lyrics to all your favorite NBB songs! Filled with pictures of the band and lyrics to their songs, this is the only way to sing along with the hottest group around.

0-545-03838-3 Naked Brothers Band: Chapter Book #1 Cry Wolff
No one knows the pressures of stardom better than the Naked Brothers Band. Award shows, live concerts, screaming fans, and music videos can take their toll—especially when you're not even old enough to drive! No one said being a star would be easy, but when the Video Music Awards, a terrifying prediction, and a demanding Transylvanian video director all slam the band, things start to crack. Will they be able to pull through? Or will the pressure prove to be too much to take?

. . . And stay tuned for more to come!